This edition published by Parragon Books Ltd in 2016

Parragon Books Ltd
Chartist House
15–17 Trim Street
Bath BA1 1HA, UK
www.parragon.com

Adapted from the original story by Jim McCann
Illustrated by Ron Lim and Chris Sotomayor

ISBN 978-1-4748-3603-6

Printed in China

Hi! I'm your friendly neighbourhood
Spider-Man. That kid back there is Peter Parker –
that's also me. See, before I became Spider-Man
I was a normal teenager. Nobody looked twice
at me. But one day, when I was in a science
lab, a radioactive spider bit me –
giving me incredible
super powers and
changing my
life forever.

Now, I live a double life. I'm still Peter Parker, the high-school student, but I'm also the Incredible Spider-Man. I can climb walls, shoot webs and lift 10-tonne trucks. I have to do homework *and* catch bad guys! I never really get a day off. After all, you never know when someone will need Spidey's help....

So even when I hit the beach for some rest
and relaxation, I'm still on lifeguard duty!

Uh-oh, I should have known I might bump into Sandman here.
This guy means trouble. Looks like I'm on Super Hero duty today, too!

"Hey, Sandman, this is a crime-free zone.
Can't you let these people build
sandcastles in peace?"

Well, at least I've got my new friend to help me.
All we need to do is keep Sandman tied
up until the police arrive.

Now *that's* what I call a sandcastle!

"Thanks for your help, buddy, you could make a great hero one
day. High five for teamwork!"

Eww – instead of a high five, I get a sneeze in the face.
Well, no one ever said being a Super Hero was glamorous!

Next morning I feel way worse than usual. My head hurts, and my throat is so scratchy – maybe I got some sand in it at the beach? I feel so ... so....

"*Achoooo!*"

Oh no, that little kid must have made me sick. But Spider-Man can't catch a bug – I have too many bad guys to battle. Even worse, I have school today!

At school, my friend Mary Jane tells me off.

"Peter Parker! What are you doing here?" she says. "You should be in bed, resting. You could have the flu!"

"I'm fine, MJ," I reply, sniffling. "It's just a cold. Nothing to worry about, honestly."

Just then, we're interrupted by a familiar voice. "Don't worry about puny Parker, Mary Jane...."

It's Flash Thompson, the school bully. And he's wearing a silly Spider-Man mask.

"Spider-Man is here to protect you! Besides, that wimp's cold probably wouldn't even hurt a bug," Flash laughs.

"Peter Parker is more like Spider-Man than you could ever be!" Mary Jane replies angrily.

If only she knew that the real Spider-Man costume was right here in my backpack!

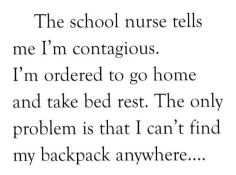

The school nurse tells
me I'm contagious.
I'm ordered to go home
and take bed rest. The only
problem is that I can't find
my backpack anywhere....

And there's more trouble –
Doctor Octopus is heading
this way! There's no time to find
my costume, but it turns out that
there is more than one Spider-
Man in Midtown High today.

"Interesting new costume, web-slinger," Doc says when he sees me. "I guess being a hero doesn't pay much money, after all."

"You should ask for a raise yourself, Doc," I say, trying to avoid his tentacles. "You need a haircut!"

"Enough jokes! Let's see what sort of haircut Spider-Man has under his mask."

I'm way too sick to stand up to Doc's tentacle attacks. He rips my mask off....

"Is that Peter Parker?" I hear Mary Jane cry.

Doctor Octopus is furious when he sees my face, and throws me to the ground. It's really not my day.

"A child? What kind of trick is this?" Doc shouts. "Spider-Man! Come out wherever you are and fight like a man. Stop hiding behind these schoolkids!"

Doc starts smashing
up the school building,
trying to find the 'real'
Spider-Man. I need
to stop this, fast. I'm
putting everyone in
danger – including
Mary Jane.

I crawl away
from the battle ...
and luckily find my
backpack! I hope
the right costume
makes a difference.

Once Doctor Octopus has been dealt with, it's time for Spider-Man to exit and Peter Parker to return....

"Peter?" Mary Jane calls. "Peter, where are you? Somebody help us over here!"

Even Flash seems concerned.

"Hey guys, I'm over here. I'm okay, really," I say.

"We were so worried!" Mary Jane says.

"You missed all the action!" Flash adds. "Spider-Man showed up and saved the day. You know, the real one."

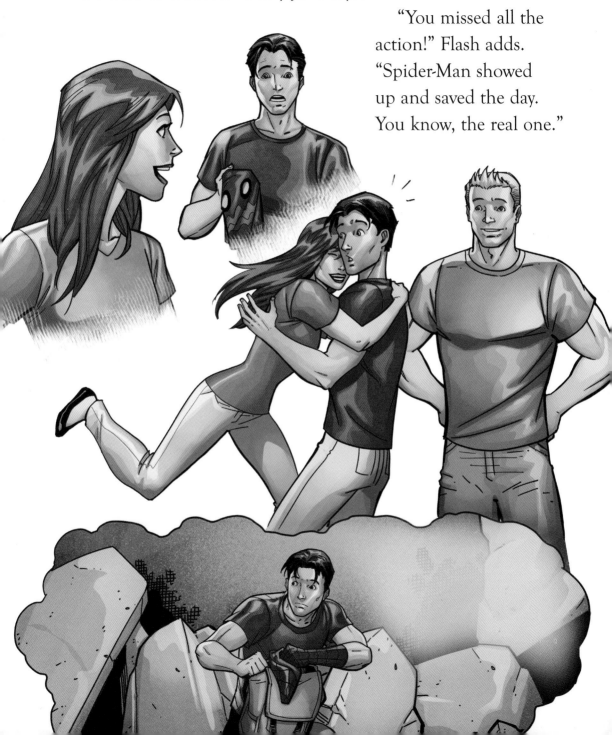

"Speaking of Spider-Man, I think this belongs to you,"
I say, handing Flash his mask.

"No, you keep it," Flash replies. "MJ was right – you were more
Spider-Man today than I could ever be."

"And you're not doing it again," Mary Jane adds, snatching the
mask out of my hands. "You could have been seriously hurt,
Peter Parker. What were you thinking?"

At home, Aunt May orders me to rest up. "I saw what happened on the news," she says. "I'm proud of you for protecting your friends, but in future, find a safer way, you hear me?"

"Yes, Aunt May," I reply.

So, maybe I should have taken a sick day. But sometimes, even a hero has to find the strength to keep going, to remember he has the responsibility to protect the ones he loves. And after all ...

... the Spider is mightier than the bug!